PICKLE FACE

Perfectly Imperfect

Jennifer Williams

Print ISBN: 978-1-09830-726-4

eBook ISBN: 978-1-09830-727-1

PICKLE FACE:
Spring Break vacation

"Woohoo! Spring break!" I yelled. Can you say excited?!? After being in school and working so hard, it was finally time for a vacation. It was the first day of spring break. We were all excited—me, Mom, Dad, and my little sister Emily.

We were going on a mini trip to Water Land. We began our trip on the road—singing songs, sleeping, and even making restroom stops on the way. "It is about three hours away," Dad said.

"Three hours?" Emily sighed.

"We'll be there in no time," Mom said. "Just relax."

Off we went. Before long, Dad woke us up saying, "Kids—look! You are going to love this. The first thing I saw was water, colors, rides, and a bunch of people. I was instantly excited with what I saw ahead of me. I don't think I've ever seen so many people in my entire life. I was a bit nervous.

My mom grabbed my hand and said, "Come on, Sam, its ok." We headed towards the water. As we began to walk, I felt my nerves leave instantly once I saw the big water slides and the bright colors. I was so excited, I started to pull Mom to the water slides.

"Come on, Mom, let's go!" I said excitedly. Mom stopped me right there and told Emily and I that we had to eat first before we got in the water. Emily and I sat down and stuffed the sandwiches down so quickly, I began to gag. After we finished, we were anxious to play. As we headed to the slides, the park employees told us that the park was closing for the day in thirty minutes. I begged Mom and Dad to let us get in the water before closing time, but their response was, "We will have to wait until tomorrow, and then we'll have so much fun."

We finally made it to the hotel where we were staying for the entire spring break. It was time for Emily and me to get cleaned up and have dinner, so we could be well-rested for our first day of fun tomorrow. "Oh boy!" I yelled with excitement. "This is going to be a long night thinking about the water park!"

"Not to mention all the loud noises from the hallway from the other people also here for spring break!" Mom said. Now, I was even more excited to meet and make friends with the other kids. I climbed into bed but couldn't sleep. Emily made "woosh" noises with her mouth, until, finally, she fell asleep. Then, I quickly dozed off.

My sleep didn't last long, as I kept waking up every hour, peeping out the window to see if it was morning yet. Finally, I just decided to go back to bed. I woke up to the sound of the alarm. Suddenly, I heard, "Beep. Beep. Beep." Mom was yelling, "It's time for breakfast, kids."

"No, Mom! I'm tired," I responded to her as I looked out the window, rubbing my face. I gasped, still rubbing my face.

"What's wrong son"? Dad asked.

"Uhm…oh…oh…no…no…nothing," I said anxiously. I ran to the bathroom to wash up for breakfast, and on my chin, there was a pimple. "Ahh!!!!" I yelled.

Mom asked again, "What's wrong?" Worried, she looked and said, "Oh honey, it's just a pimple."

"No Mom, it's not!" I yelled. "I can't go to the water park like this."

"No one will even notice it. Just leave it alone." Mom said.

All the while, I was thinking about the pretty girl I saw when I looked out the window this morning. All I could think was, "What if she sees? Will she make fun of me.?"

"Wait! I have an idea! I can just wear my jacket and zip it all the way up and then no one will notice. Great idea, right Mom?"

"Oh no, honey. Then everyone will notice that you are wearing a jacket at a water park," Mom said.

"Not to mention, it's almost summertime." Dad added.

"Oh, brother, I'll play with you!" Emily said as she grabbed my hand and smiled.

Off to the water we went. As we began playing, it felt like the world was against me. When I looked up, I saw four bigger kids approaching Emily and me. They were all pointing and laughing, and they began to shout, "Look at that thing on his face!"

'Oh no—the pimple,' I thought. I didn't realize they were talking about the kid behind me until they walked closer and then passed me. Whew! That was close. Emily turned around and pointed, shouting, "It's a booger on his face!"

"No Emily, it's not polite to point." I told her.

We walked away and went to get into the pool. "Oh, no. Hey, you." I heard someone talking. I turned around. It was the lifeguard.

"Are you talking to me?" I asked.

"Yes," he said, "If you are getting in the pool, all boys must take off their shirts." he said, pointing at the rules sign hanging on the fence.

Just then, as I was removing my shirt, I heard a group of girls a few feet ahead of me, laughing and pointing in my direction. "Ewww...put it back on!" they shouted.

"Oh no, not again." I sighed. This was not turning out to be fun, as I looked back and realized they weren't talking about me, but about a kid behind me. He was pulling of his bandages to get in the water. "That was close," I muttered.

Splash, splash, splash, we began to play. We played until lunchtime. We could hear Mom seemingly a mile away when she called us in. "Okay kids, it's time to eat!"

We ran off to the table where Mom had prepared pizza, chips, and a snack. We sat down to eat and talked about all the fun we were having.

Emily loudly announced that she needed to use the restroom.

"I'll take her, Mom. Let's go!" I said. We ran around the building. Emily went to the girl's and I went to the boy's bathrooms. As I approached the stall, I looked over into the mirror and immediately saw more pimples. More pimples!? Oh no. I began to run out. Then, I remembered Emily and turned back to get her. As I turned around, I saw a beautiful girl approaching the restroom. It was the same girl I saw the first day we arrived. She was standing right across from me. I panicked. I couldn't let her see me like this. What should I do? I hid behind the building, hoping she would leave soon.

At that moment, Emily came out and yelled, "Samuel! Where are you!?" The girl, with her friends, no scars no marks, so beautiful, was still standing there. I gazed at her for so long, I eventually felt Emily tugging on me and asking, "What's wrong? What is it?"

I replied, "Oh, nothing. Let's go get back to our lunch."

When we arrived back, Dad was reading a book and Mom was on the phone, chatting about how much fun we were having. In the background, I was thinking about how to get rid of these pimples and how to avoid being seen like this by the girl of my dreams.

"Ok kids let's go back to the room," Dad told us.

"Yes, that's a good idea." I said, relieved.

"Why the urgency to get back, Sam?" Mom asked.

"Umm…well, Mom look at my face!"

"Oh, honey. They're just pimples. It's normal."

"Normal? There's got to be a solution. I'm starting to look like a half-eaten pickle!"

After we washed up for the day, Dad suggested we go for ice cream down in the lobby. I thought I had seen it all until I got downstairs. There were more fun and games, but I couldn't dare be seen like this. It was time for ice cream, and the line was long.

"Come on, guys," Dad said. "Let's get in line."

"I'll stay here. Just grab me something." I told him.

"No, son," Dad said, "You'll have to come pick your own ice cream. There are so many flavors."

When I finally decided to get in line, there were so many flavors to choose from. There was vanilla, strawberry, peach, coconut, watermelon, apple, blueberry, banana, cotton candy, root beer, raspberry, cheesecake, red velvet, chocolate, Oreo, and lemon.

"So many flavors!!!!" I shouted. "Can I have three?"

"Sure," Dad said with no hesitation, as if he were relieved. I got in line for ice cream. As I chose my flavors, someone behind me suggested I try chocolate and cheesecake, because they were her favorite. It didn't take me long before I recognized the voice talking to me, so I turned around and saw perfection. I stood there, dazed at the beautiful girl who spoke to me.

"Are you ok?" she asked.

"Uh, uh, yes, yes, I'm fine." I responded as she laughed. "Hi, my name is Samuel! What's your name?" I asked.

She responded, "Rebecca—"

"Next!" the ice cream man yelled before she could finish "What's your flavor, kid?"

"I'll just have two flavors—chocolate and vanilla please."

"Great choice." Dad said, smiling.

After we ate our ice cream, we went off to play games. First, we played musical chairs, because that was my sister's favorite game. We also played hide-and-seek with the rest of the kids at the park. We even played a game of hip-hop squares. In that game, we couldn't step on the squares that lit up with musical notes. That was one of my favorites. Hours later, Rebecca invited me to join her and some friends. It turns out she was on a field trip with friends from school and some of her family. "Sure," I said. "Let me ask my parents if it's okay with them."

"Sure, of course!" Mom said, excited that I was finally making friends. "Have fun but don't go too far. It's getting late and we only have a few days left."

A few days? How? Where did the time go? As I walked away to get back to Rebecca, I realized I had made a friend. Wait—did she see my face? I started to panic, but then I remembered Mom said no one is perfect ('*Except Rebecca*,' I thought). Back with her group of friends, we all sat down on the benches. My heart felt as if it were just about to leave my body. My palms got all sweaty. Rebecca introduced me to everyone as her new friend. Everyone was so nice and excited to meet me. In that moment, I realized this wasn't as bad as I thought.

We laughed, joked, and finished our ice cream. "Hey guys, would you all like to play a game of Uno?" I asked. Everyone answered yes. Everyone except for Rebecca, who looked as if she didn't hear me talking to her. '*Oh, no*,' I thought. "Maybe she doesn't like Uno, or maybe she doesn't know what it is. I leaned over and asked her again.

She grabbed her ear and said, "I'm sorry. Did you say something? My hearing aids! I need to switch it out."

'Hearing aid? So, nobody's perfect,' I thought to myself. As the game of Uno came to an end, I heard Mom yelling and waving to get my attention.

"It's time to go! Say goodbye to your friends for tonight."

As we headed back to the room, I couldn't help thinking about Rebecca's hearing aid. As I was telling my Mom about it, she said, "See! I told you—nobody's perfect."

Dad added, "We all have flaws—some seen and others unseen, and you'll never know what flaws other people have until you get to know them."

"So, did you have fun?" Mom asked.

"Oh, yes, and I can hardly wait for tomorrow. Woohoo!" I answered, yelling and running down the long colorful hallway.

"Shh…quiet!" Dad said. "Not so loud. It's just about bedtime, and people are settling down."

In the bathroom, as Emily and I were brushing our teeth, I notice my pimples were gone. I was so thrilled, I forgot to wash my face.

"Goodnight, Mom. Goodnight, Dad." I said. "I can't wait until tomorrow to see my friends again."

Beep! beep! Beep! There was the sound of the alarm, and Mom calling for us to come have breakfast so we could get an early start on the day. Dad had a surprise planned for us at Water Land. "So, what are we going to do first?" Emily asked.

Mom answered, "How about we pick souvenirs—one for each of us to remember our spring break. That sounds fun, right?"

Off we went to store after store. All I could think about was getting back to the park with my new friends. Finally, back to hotel, everyone changed into water clothes and then there was a knock at the door.

"I got it." Dad said, then called out, "Sam, you have company."

It was Rebecca and her friends. "Hi Sam!" they said. "Are you ready to go to the water park?"

"Yeah sure. Oh, wait. I can't right now. We have plans. I will have to catch up with you all later."

"Ok, that's fine." Rebecca said.

"Hurry! We have to go!" Dad yelled as he was heading towards the elevator. "I have something planned for us that I think will be very exciting."

As we stepped off the elevator, we ran into Rebecca's parents. Mom invited them to come along with us. As we approached the other side of the park, we read a sign that promised even more fun:

Horse Riding
Sack racing
Apple-bobbing
Dart throwing, and so
much more

We were having so much fun, I didn't notice there was a smaller horse standing off by himself while the handler was hand feeding him. I was very curious as to why, so Dad walked Emily and I over. The handler asked if we would like to feed him. I was a bit nervous, but Emily was ready, so she fed him. I asked why this horse couldn't ride. The handler explained to me that he was blind since birth. I felt awfully sad for him, but Dad assured me that he was okay and cared for by many people.

"Ok kids let's go. Apple-bobbing is about to begin, and then we should definitely try sack racing." Dad said. We stood in line, waiting for our turn. As more people gathered, the scorekeeper went over the rules and told us that there would be a prize for the winner.

The game started, and before I knew it, I was up next. Walking to take my place, I noticed all the other competition. Suddenly, I felt extremely nervous. Looking back at the crowd, I heard Dad yell, "You've got this, son!" Even though I lost, I still had a blast. Dad said to me, "That's the spirit son," while laughing and talking about how much fun the trip had been.

While waiting to eat dinner, Emily went on and on about how much fun she was having and how she didn't want to leave. Just then, Mom said "Ok, dinner is ready."

"Don't worry, Emily. We have one more day before we leave." Dad replied. "Boy, how time flies when you're having fun."

I wasn't ready to go. I just made awesome friends who weren't as perfect as I thought and that was very awesome because I fit in. I realized I didn't have to be ashamed of the way I looked, and that was very reassuring. Mom always told me that "no one is perfect." We all have flaws, and things of which we are ashamed or embarrassed, but we shouldn't be. We are "perfectly imperfect" and that's what makes us all unique.

After dinner, Mom allowed us to stay up until 10 p.m. We watched movies and ate popcorn until we started to drift off and eventually went to bed. The next morning of our last day at Water Land, I decided to spend the day with Rebecca and her friends. After breakfast, I asked if I could go downstairs to the pool.

"Sure, but don't forget your sunscreen." Dad said as he finished his breakfast and another chapter in his book.

As I was leaving, Mom shouted, "I'll be down with Emily soon! We just have to get ready, but you be careful."

"I will Mom. See you soon."

Approaching the pool, I saw Rebecca already in the water playing with some friends. She turned and saw me and invited me over to join them in a race down the slides. It was so much fun as we were twirling down the slide. Rebecca grabbed her ear and said, "Oh no! I lost my hearing aid!" We quickly went to the park manager and asked if he could help find it. He told us that the staff would let us know if they did. As the day went on, the park manager called her over. They had found her hearing aid! She was very happy. We ran off and continued to play. At snack time, Rebecca's mom called out, "Hey Sam, come join us!" She said she made their favorite chocolate peanut butter brownies that sounded delicious!

"Don't mind if I do," I agreed.

After lunch, M om gathered us together to take pictures and I realized the time was drawing near for us to leave and head back home. I didn't want to leave! I was having the most fun I'd had in a long time, and I made friends that I probably wouldn't see for a while. It turned out Rebecca lived three hours away. Even though I was bummed about that, I smiled and took pictures. Rebecca suggested our parents exchange numbers so we could keep in touch and make plans for the summer.

"Great idea!" I said, so they did.

Dad packed up the car while we said our goodbyes. On our way home, Mom asked what the most fun thing about the trip was. I quickly answered and said meeting new people, but the most important thing was seeing that no one is perfect and in one way or another we are all different.